The Ordinary Miracle of a Purple Balloon

Written By Patricia A. Langer

Illustrated By Rachael Budd

AuthorHouse™
1663 Liberty Drive
Bloomington, IN 47403
www.authorhouse.com
Phone: 1 (800) 839-8640

Published by AuthorHouse 03/22/2019

ISBN: 978-1-7283-0410-6 (sc)
ISBN: 978-1-7283-0412-0 (hc)
ISBN: 978-1-7283-0411-3 (e)

Library of Congress Control Number: 2019902998

Print information available on the last page.

authorHOUSE®

DEDICATION

With an eternity of gratitude
I dedicate this book to:

Holly and Beau Dubina, my
niece and nephew, who blessed
me with the love of books.

Rachael Budd, my illustrator. Your
talent, dedication and burst of
color goes beyond measure.

Clarkstown High School North,
New City, NY

Please take the time to listen to the song,
"Ordinary Miracle" by Sarah McLachlan

It was such a happy evening. A prelude
filled with laughter, smiles and a reason
to celebrate. From high above the crowd,
I could see that the night was gloriously
surrounded by the synergy of caps and
gowns and balloons just like me.

Yes, purple balloons! Balloons by the hundreds filled the sky. Each one was delicately grasped by families too proud to go unrecognized.

A Commencement of sorts and the auspicious
Pomp and Circumstance was just beginning.
Somewhere in the afterglow of that evening
one special balloon slipped away from
all the festive hoopla. That was me!

So it was, on that June night, that I began my unexpected journey to an unknown land. Diminished by the sunset, I could feel myself floating against the complimentary mixture of red and orange as it reflected above the sky.

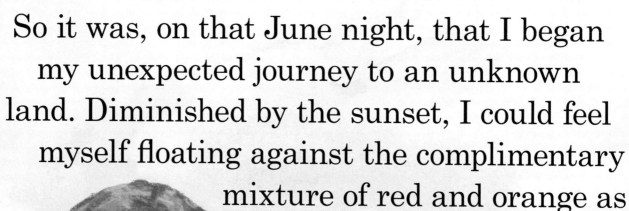

As a balloon, I experienced a feeling unlike any I ever imagined. It was like being in an elevator that didn't stop.

It became evident that I was meant to
serve a larger purpose in the shadows
of the sunset. Or was this to be just
an **Ordinary Miracle** of today?

Unlike all the
purple balloons, I
was the shiny one.
I was the one called
Clark North.

I reflected the mylar of hard work and dedication in a star filled sky of personal success pushed by the breeze.

I stood apart from all the rest because I had the strength of a ram. My large curled horns became a status symbol in the constellation of the universe. Yet as I floated up to the sky, I seemed to lose my "ramifidence" (ram confidence).

In its place occupied a feeling of helplessness and uncertainty. I didn't know where I was going. In this place, so far away, the ride was sure to become a life changing event.

In that time period I came to realize something profound. For the first time I learned that when your feet don't touch the earth, you can't feel the worries that hurt. A deep sense of peace enveloped me.

Night after night and day after day this non-stop flight and cosmic consciousness enlightened my purpose beside the stars. This nebulae of material with the helium of my soul kept my spirit soaring. I was flying for 19 days and a total of 150 miles.

I felt safe in a place high above the clouds. Up here, in the vast sky, there was no map to follow and no path to show the way. Everything was different and this summer was everything! I simply journeyed by the **Ordinary Miracle** of the day.

After many days and many miles of traveling, I grew tired. I felt so much smaller than the warm yellow stars I once touched. Gradually, I found myself brushing the green summer tree tops. Lower and lower I descended. I tried desperately to rise above the quagmire below, but failed, due to the lack of helium.

So it was, one late afternoon in July, that my journey had come to an end. It was there, on a green lawn in Woodstock that I landed. I was carpeted by the gravitational distance that brought us together. So soft was the carpet. So brilliant was the sunset.

Little did I realize that the universe truly saved the best for last. Leaving the sky to remember the "Extra" **Ordinary Miracle** of each day.

Author's Note ♪♪♪

It is my wish that <u>The Ordinary Miracle of a Purple Balloon</u> serves as both a mirror and a window. May whatever you project to those in the world, be reflected back to you, in the nicest of ways. People come into our lives for a reason, a season, or a lifetime. There's no telling where the helium inside your mylar will take you. Just allow the orchestration to guide you in unexpected ways.

Always keep a song in your heart.

"Sing" cerely,

Patricia A. Langer
a.k.a. Balloon Lady

Printed in the United States
By Bookmasters